This Ladybird Book belongs to:

~~SCHOOL LIBRARY~~ SCHOOL LIBRARY

Thank You

to Kimia Shiri
for this book

This Ladybird retelling
by
Joan Stimson

Published by Ladybird Books Ltd
80 Strand London WC2R 0RL
A Penguin Company
15 17 19 20 18 16 14

© LADYBIRD BOOKS LTD 1993

Printed in Italy

Chicken Licken

*illustrated
by
PETULA STONE*

based on a traditional folk tale

Once upon a time there was a little
chick called Chicken Licken.

One day, as he was playing, an acorn
fell on his head.

"Help!" thought Chicken Licken.
"The sky is falling down!"

And he ran off to tell the King.

On the way, Chicken Licken met
Henny Penny.

"Oh! Henny Penny!" cried Chicken
Licken. "The sky is falling down and
I'm off to tell the King."

"Then I shall come too," said Henny
Penny.

So Chicken Licken and Henny Penny
hurried off to find the King.

On the way, Chicken Licken and
Henny Penny met Cocky Locky.

"Oh! Cocky Locky!" cried Chicken
Licken. "The sky is falling down and
we're off to tell the King."

"Then I shall come too," said Cocky Locky.

So Chicken Licken, Henny Penny and Cocky Locky hurried off to find the King.

On the way, Chicken Licken, Henny Penny and Cocky Locky met Ducky Lucky.

"Oh! Ducky Lucky!" cried Chicken Licken. "The sky is falling down and we're off to tell the King."

"Then I shall come too," said Ducky Lucky.

So Chicken Licken, Henny Penny,
Cocky Locky and Ducky Lucky
hurried off to find the King.

On the way, Chicken Licken, Henny Penny, Cocky Locky and Ducky Lucky met Drakey Lakey.

"Oh! Drakey Lakey!" cried Chicken Licken. "The sky is falling down and we're off to tell the King."

"Then I shall come too," said Drakey Lakey.

So Chicken Licken, Henny Penny, Cocky Locky, Ducky Lucky and Drakey Lakey hurried off to find the King.

On the way, Chicken Licken, Henny Penny, Cocky Locky, Ducky Lucky and Drakey Lakey met Goosey Loosey.

"Oh! Goosey Loosey!" cried Chicken Licken. "The sky is falling down and we're off to tell the King."

"Then I shall come too," said Goosey Loosey.

So Chicken Licken, Henny Penny, Cocky Locky, Ducky Lucky, Drakey Lakey and Goosey Loosey hurried off to find the King.

On the way, Chicken Licken, Henny Penny, Cocky Locky, Ducky Lucky, Drakey Lakey and Goosey Loosey met Turkey Lurkey.

"Oh! Turkey Lurkey!" cried Chicken Licken. "The sky is falling down and we're off to tell the King."

"Then I shall come too," said Turkey Lurkey.

So Chicken Licken, Henny Penny, Cocky Locky, Ducky Lucky, Drakey Lakey, Goosey Loosey and Turkey Lurkey hurried off to find the King.

But on the way, they met Foxy Loxy!

"Good morning," said Foxy Loxy. "Where are you all going in such a hurry?"

"Oh! Foxy Loxy!" cried Chicken Licken. "The sky is falling down and we're off to tell the King."

"Follow me," said Foxy Loxy. "I know just where to find the King."

So Chicken Licken, Henny Penny, Cocky Locky, Ducky Lucky, Drakey Lakey, Goosey Loosey and Turkey Lurkey all followed Foxy Loxy.

But he didn't take them to the King.
He led them straight to his den,
where his wife and all the little foxes
were waiting for their dinner.

Then the foxes ate up Chicken Licken, Henny Penny, Cocky Locky, Ducky Lucky, Drakey Lakey, Goosey Loosey and Turkey Lurkey.

And Chicken Licken never did find the King to tell him that the sky was falling down!